Maisie
Hitchins

For William

~HW

For Yolande with love

~ML

STRIPES PUBLISHING LIMITED
An imprint of the Little Tiger Group
1 Coda Studios, 189 Munster Road,
London SW6 6AW

A paperback original
First published in Great Britain in 2015

ISBN: 978-1-84715-513-9

A CIP catalogue record for this book is available from the British Library.

Printed and bound in the UK.

4 6 8 10 9 7 5 3

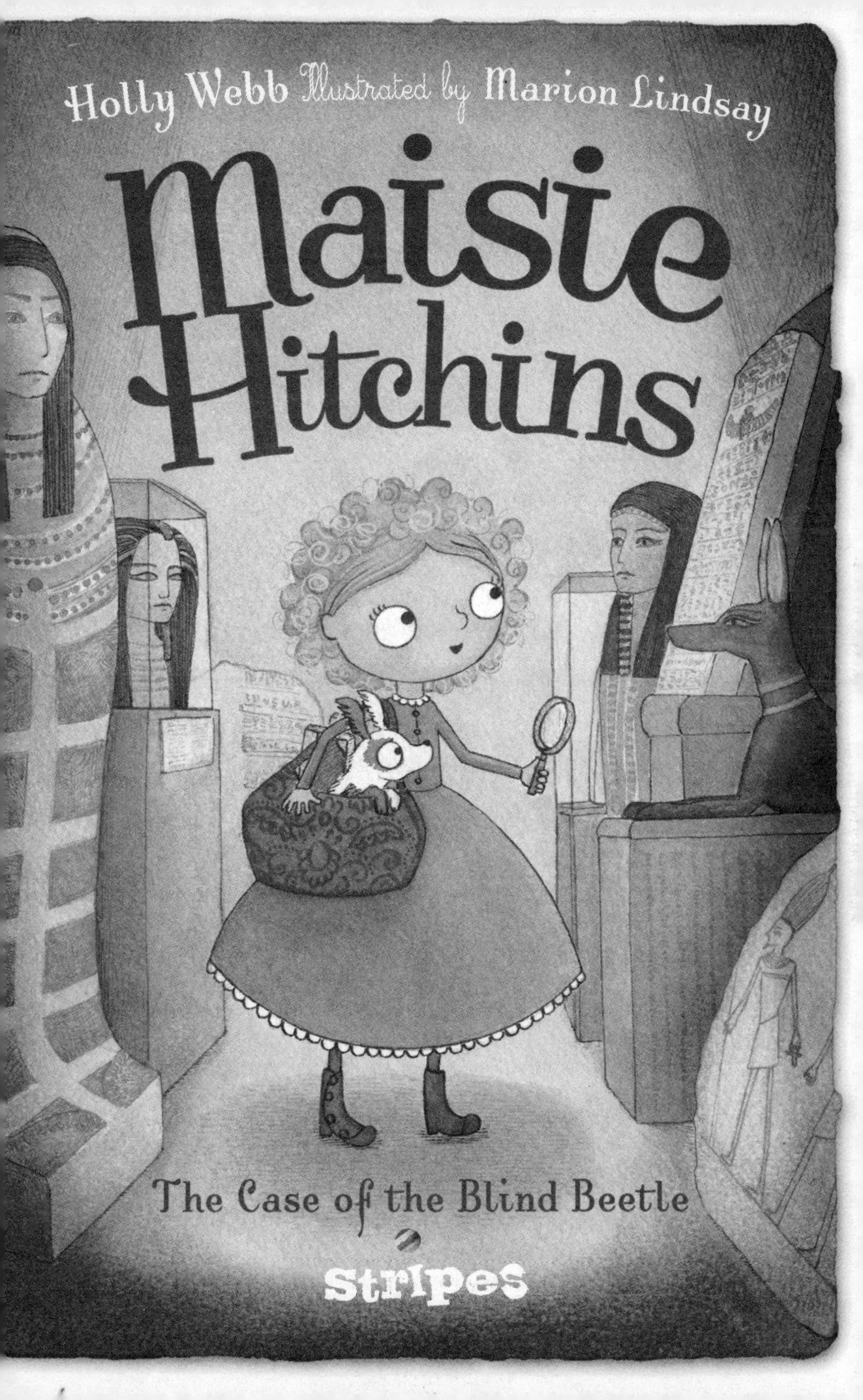
Holly Webb Illustrated by Marion Lindsay
Maisie Hitchins
The Case of the Blind Beetle
stripes

31 Albion Street, London

Attic:

Maisie's grandmother and Sally the maid

Third floor:

Miss Lane's rooms

Second floor:

Mr Smith's rooms

First floor:

Professor Tobin's rooms

Ground floor:

Entrance hall, sitting room and dining room

Basement:

Maisie's room, kitchen and yard entrance

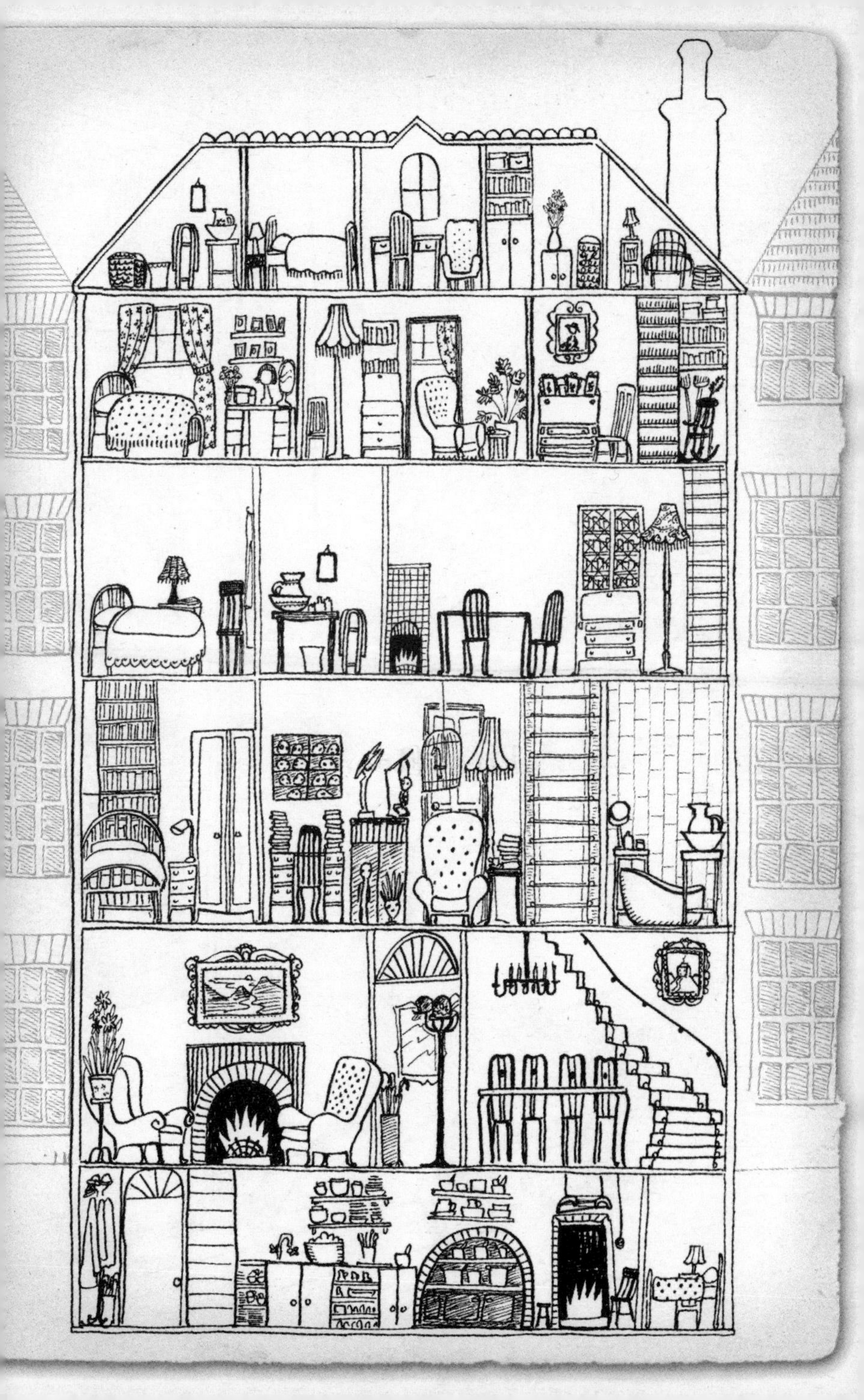

Maisie hurried up the stairs from the kitchen, muttering to herself. "I'm coming! For heaven's sake, I'm coming! I've only just sat down, you know." And that was after making *all* the beds, and washing up from breakfast. Her tea would get cold.

Eddie, her little brown and white dog, galloped up the steps in front, nearly tripping her up. He sniffed hard at the door and let out a flurry of suspicious yelps.

"It could be someone coming to rent the second-floor rooms," Maisie told him, suddenly hopeful. She smoothed down her apron. "Shh, Eddie! We don't want to put them off."

The second-floor rooms of Gran's boarding house had been empty for a while, which meant money was tight. Maisie hadn't had a penny to spend on toffees for many weeks, and Gran looked worried all the time – there was a thin line between her eyebrows, which never went away.

But when Maisie swung open the front door, a boy was standing there with a parcel, and Maisie could see a carrier's cart waiting in the road for him.

"Hurry up, lad!" the man driving the cart called impatiently.

"Mrs Sarah Hitchins and Miss Maisie Hitchins?" the boy gabbled, thrusting the parcel at Maisie.

"Yes. That's me – I mean, I'm Maisie—"

Before she could finish her sentence, the boy was off, leaping back on to the box of the cart. The driver slapped the reins on the horse's neck and made chirruping noises to send him on his way.

Maisie stared down at the parcel in her arms. Eddie scrabbled at her skirt, yapping and trying to sniff at the cloth-wrapped bundle.

"I thought it would be for Professor Tobin," Maisie murmured. "He's always getting strange things sent from abroad. No, Eddie, you're not to bite it!" Holding the parcel up high, she walked slowly back into the hallway and pushed the door shut.

Professor Tobin's last parcel had come from a friend of his who was working somewhere in Italy, and had contained rare butterflies pinned on to a card, along with a large sausage. It had reached the professor slightly chewed...

"It really is for Gran and me. I can't tell from the writing, the label's a bit smudged, but do you think...?" Maisie suddenly broke into a run, galloping headlong down the stairs and bursting into the kitchen. "Gran! Gran! Look!"

"Whatever's the matter, Maisie?" Gran stared at her over the cup of tea she was holding.

"A parcel – for both of us! Is it... Is it from Father, do you think? The writing's smeared – I wasn't sure."

Gran put down the teacup, her hands shaking so that it jingled in its saucer. "Your father! Oh, Maisie, has he sent us something?"

"I'm not sure we'll ever be able to get into it to find out," Maisie muttered, fingering the knotted lengths of string that wound around the parcel. "I suppose he is a sailor, tying rope is part of his job. Gran, can we cut them, please? It'll take years to undo all these knots!"

Gran sniffed, obviously torn between saving the useful string and her eagerness to see what was inside the parcel. "Oh, very well!" She took the package from Maisie and peered at the label while Sally, the maid who shared the work at the boarding house, fetched the scissors. "I wonder where he sent it from..."

Maisie snipped at the knots and finally opened the parcel. She pulled out a beautiful silk shawl and a little leather pouch, together with a letter addressed to Gran. She handed it over.

"He says he decided to send me the shawl now, after all, rather than bringing it home with him, as he wanted to imagine me wearing it while he was away," Gran said, smiling as she read the letter. "And inside the pouch there's a present for you, Maisie. He says it's Egyptian, very old. From the time of the pharaohs, so the man who sold it to him in the souk in Cairo said. A souk is a market, I think. But your father isn't sure how old it really is. Anyway, he says it's a mystery, with a secret message, and maybe you can solve it with your detecting."

"He really said that?" Maisie murmured, undoing the drawstring at the top of the little pouch and tipping the contents out into her hand. She hadn't been sure what her father would think about the cases she had solved. She had written to tell him about them, but she'd had so few letters in return over the years he had been away that it was hard to tell what sort of person he was. He might have thought that her detective work was unladylike and dangerous, or (worse) just silly. But if her father had sent her a secret message to solve, it didn't sound as though he was going to try and make her stop, when he came home in a few months' time.

"It's a necklace," she said, holding up a pendant dangling on a dull gold chain. "What sort of stone is that?"

"A carnelian?" Sally suggested, leaning over to see. "It's a lovely colour, Maisie, that dark red."

"It's engraved," Maisie said, peering at the pendant in the dim light of the kitchen. "Look at these lines – is that an eye? And there are more symbols on the other side. That must be the mystery." She ran her thumb gently over the pendant and smiled to herself. Her very own mystery, from her father.

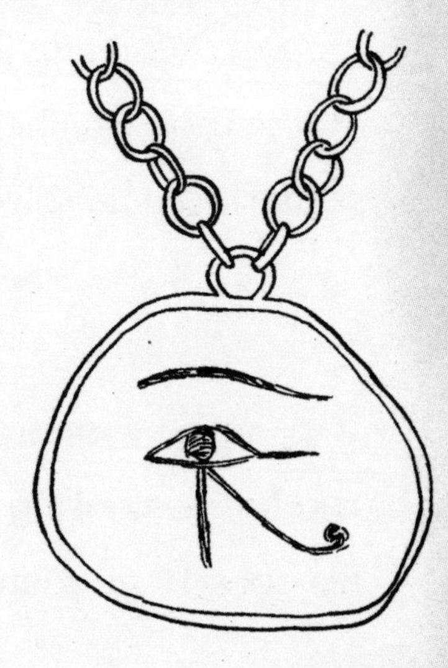

She would look at it properly later on, with the magnifying glass that Professor Tobin had given her to help with her detective work. She slipped the chain over her head and tucked the pendant under her dress, so it wouldn't get in the way while she was dusting.

"You could ask the professor what it means," Gran suggested, and Maisie nodded. Professor Tobin was sure to know or, if he didn't, he'd have a book he could look in.

But that seems like cheating, somehow, Maisie thought. She would wait a while and see if she could solve the mystery by herself.

"Cup of tea, Professor?" Maisie asked, carefully balancing the tray as she opened his door. He usually had some tea and biscuits at this time of the afternoon.

The professor peered out from behind his newspaper, his huge white eyebrows drawn together so that he looked rather grumpy.

Maisie paused by the door, wondering if she shouldn't have disturbed him.

"Oh, come in, come in," the professor growled. "I'm sorry, Maisie, it's not you I'm cross with. A cup of tea might cheer me up."

"Is there something wrong, sir?" Maisie asked him. She'd seen the professor look worried before, but he was always friendly and polite.

"This!" The professor shook the newspaper. "Utter nonsense! Look, Maisie!"

Maisie put down the tea tray on the little table next to his chair and peered at the tiny print. The article seemed to be about someone called Lord Dacre.

"Oh! Egypt! My father has just been there. He wrote to us from Cairo." She started to read aloud. "Lord Dacre has discovered an amazing set of royal tombs… Full of precious artefacts… Solid gold statues! Goodness, they're a bit strange-looking." She frowned at the drawing printed in the paper, trying to work out the best angle to look at it from.

"Leggy Dacre has only discovered them because he has more money than he knows what to do with!" the professor snapped. "Anyone can go and find Egyptian tombs if they have a few spare million. He's had an army of workers out there digging. Would have been more of a miracle if they *hadn't* found anything!"

"Do you know him, then, Professor?" Maisie asked, wondering why the professor called Lord Dacre *Leggy*.

"I was at university with him," Professor Tobin said, shaking the newspaper again. "He's a friend of mine, really. I'm just a grumpy old man, Maisie. I'd like to have millions to spend on an expedition, that's all. Your father was in Egypt, did you say?"

"Yes, he sent me a present, look." Maisie carefully pulled her beautiful pendant over her head, hoping it would cheer the professor up. She wouldn't mind if he solved the mystery of the pictures, if it made him feel better.

The professor held it gently. "This is thousands of years old, Maisie. What a treasure! You're a lucky girl. These are hieroglyphics on the underside. Picture writing. I'm not an Egyptian expert, though, so I'm afraid I don't know what it means."

"My father said it was a mystery for me – to work out what it said," Maisie explained. "It's like a secret code."

"Excellent idea!" The professor nodded excitedly. "Tomorrow afternoon, Maisie, we shall go on an expedition of our own! To the British Museum. They have a whole Egyptian gallery there. I shall persuade your grandmother that it will be most educational. We shall see if we can find some clues."

"It's so big," Maisie murmured, as she and Professor Tobin walked through the iron gates to the British Museum. Then, as they headed across the courtyard towards the front steps, she stopped and caught the professor's sleeve. "Sir, I don't think I'm allowed in here. I can't be. It's like a palace." She was very glad she had left Eddie at home.

Professor Tobin patted her hand comfortingly. "I assure you, Maisie, you most certainly are allowed in. Why, the museum belongs to all of us!" He steered her up the broad steps and between the huge columns. "Do hurry, Maisie, I have a feeling it may snow. Look at the sky. It will be warmer inside. And now that the galleries are lit with electric light, we will have longer to look at the treasures. It used to be a terribly dark place on winter afternoons like this one. Everyone had to leave at four o'clock because you simply couldn't see a thing."

Maisie hurried after him through the entrance hall, scurrying past hundreds of marble statues all draped in the most insubstantial clothes. (Some of them were quite shocking, Maisie wasn't at all sure that Gran would approve, and on a wintry afternoon the poor things looked *frozen*.)

The professor stopped and looked back at her as they came to the opening that led into the Egyptian Galleries. He was beaming, and his smile grew wider as Maisie stared around. The galleries were large, with high ceilings, but even so the huge statues looked as though they might burst their way out.

"If that's only his head," Maisie whispered to the professor, gazing at a huge face of dark stone, "how big was the rest of him? His head is taller than me."

"He was probably sitting down," the professor pointed out helpfully. "The pharaohs often were in their statues. The museum might have managed to get all of him in here, but it would have been a squash." He led her on past the enormous statues to stand in front of a slab of grey stone set into a wooden frame with a glass top, like a painting lying flat. "Can you see it, Maisie? It's a little high… This is one of the museum's greatest treasures."

Maisie glanced at him doubtfully. The stone looked rather boring, compared to the glittering blue and gold coffins she could see further down the hall.

"This is the Rosetta Stone, Maisie – a message, you see, from the pharaoh, about taxes. I know that doesn't sound very exciting, but the important thing is that it's in three languages. This is how we learned to translate the Egyptian picture writing, the hieroglyphs!"

"Oh!" Maisie stood up on tiptoe to look at the stone. "The hieroglyphs are the bit at the top?"

"Yes. Until this was found, scholars had hardly a clue what the ancient language meant – but this stone has ancient Greek writing at the bottom and the newer Egyptian script in the middle. So they could work out some of the picture signs by comparing all three." Professor Tobin sighed and stroked his hand over the glass. "This stone is two thousand years old, Maisie – and half the exhibits in this gallery are much, much older. You know, when the stone was found, it had been built into a wall? What if no one had seen it, hmmm? We might never have known..."

Maisie peered at the hieroglyphs, wondering if she would recognize any of them from the engraving on her pendant. "Those are birds! And – is that a man with a bucket on his head? Professor, this must have taken ages to write in." She frowned, imagining trying to write a letter to her father using all these fiddly little drawings.

"I don't think most people could write in it," the professor agreed. "It was more for special occasions and announcements, not sending a note to the butcher complaining about the sausages."

"I can't see anything that looks like the symbol on my necklace," Maisie said, gazing at the squiggly drawings.

"No..." the professor agreed, as he started walking on down the gallery. "We need to ask someone, I think. I know a few of the curators, though Egyptology isn't my subject. I wonder if anyone is around..."

"Scruffy!" Maisie jumped as someone bellowed behind them, and the professor nearly fell into a sarcophagus.

"Good Lord. Leggy!" the professor cried, as a huge man seized him by the hand, and then shook it violently up and down.

"What on earth are you doing here, Scruffy?" the man demanded. "Didn't know you were interested in Egypt! Finally going to admit that the greatest civilization the world has ever known is a bit more interesting than mouldy old South American animals?"

Maisie saw the professor take a very deep breath, which made his moustache flap, but he only smiled politely. "I am interested in everything, Leggy," he answered, with a slight bow. "I was just explaining the history of the Rosetta Stone to my young friend here, Miss Hitchins. Maisie, this is Lord Dacre. I – ahem – mentioned him to you yesterday…"

"Oh!" Of course – this was the professor's friend from university, Maisie realized. The one who had millions to spend on digging up half of Egypt. Now that she looked, she could see he was particularly smartly dressed and he was very brown, as though he had been out in the sun a great deal. He also had the most immensely long legs – it was obvious where his nickname had come from.

"I'm very pleased to meet you, sir." She curtseyed. "The professor showed me the newspaper article about your finds."

Lord Dacre frowned very slightly, and

Maisie wondered if he didn't like to be reminded that his old friend was a professor, and he was not. Or perhaps he just wasn't used to being introduced to girls in shabby dresses. Maisie had put on a lace collar that her friend Alice had given her, so as to look as smart as possible for their outing, but her dress was still obviously rather old and worn.

"Charmed to meet you, young lady," he murmured. "And may I introduce my secretary, Mr Travers. Travers, this is Scruffy Tobin. Old friend. Mad collector of strange creatures..."

"Actually, my lord, I've read Professor Tobin's work on the rituals of the South American tribes." The thin young man who had been hovering behind Lord Dacre stepped forward and bowed to the professor and Maisie, a smile splitting his tanned face.

“Have you read it, Miss Hitchins?” he asked politely. “It’s a fascinating work.”

“No, sir, but the professor has shown me many of the strange things he brought back with him from the Americas,” Maisie said, smiling. She liked Mr Travers at once, and it was nice of him to suggest that she might have read something so difficult. Although she wasn't sure that Lord Dacre was very pleased. He looked quite annoyed that his secretary clearly admired old Scruffy Tobin.

"Are you here to discuss giving some of your beautiful new finds to the museum, Leggy?" Professor Tobin put in quickly. "That blue enamelled death mask looks truly exquisite, even in the drawing in the newspaper."

Lord Dacre suddenly sagged at the shoulders and seemed to look much shorter. "No… No, Scruffy. I shall of course be making some donations to the museum, but today we are here to talk to the head curator. One of the treasures of my collection has been stolen. I came to talk to Mr Canning, to ask if he could keep an eye out for it among the sale rooms, in case anyone tries to auction it off.

And I want him to let me know if the blackguard who stole it tries to sell it directly to the museum."

"Stolen?" Maisie asked curiously, before she could stop herself. It wasn't really her place to ask, but she couldn't resist.

"My beautiful Golden Scarab," Lord Dacre pulled an embroidered handkerchief out of his pocket, and blew his nose loudly. "Gone. Disappeared. I've had the police with me all morning, but they couldn't tell me anything useful. No forced entry, they said. They had the cheek to suggest it was one of my household that took it! Piffle!"

"A scarab," Professor Tobin repeated. "A beetle?"

Maisie looked at him thoughtfully. The professor was very knowledgeable about all sorts of animals, and she had a feeling that he knew very well what a scarab was. He just wanted his old friend to enjoy knowing something that he didn't. The professor was trying to cheer him up, Maisie decided.

"Not just any beetle! *The* beetle! A sacred image for the Egyptian people, Scruffy!" Lord Dacre launched into lecturing mode, and began to pace up and down. "The great symbol of the sun! The god Ra, you know, in his aspect of Khepri, the beetle."

"Their god was a beetle?" Maisie asked in surprise, but Lord Dacre was too carried away with his lecture to listen.

"Not just any beetle," Mr Travers whispered in her ear. "A dung beetle! Er, poo, you know?"

"I most certainly don't!" Maisie glanced at him suspiciously, thinking that he must be teasing her.

"It's the truth, I promise you. The dung beetles roll balls of dung to their nests to lay their eggs in. And that reminded the Egyptians of the sun moving across the sky as a great fiery ball."

"They got all that from *dung*?" Maisie muttered.

"Well, so we think," Mr Travers agreed. "Ah, excuse me, my lord." He bowed hastily to Lord Dacre, who had noticed that they weren't listening and was glaring at them both. "I was trying to explain the background to Miss Hitchins. The importance of the god Khepri."

"And you found this precious scarab on your recent expedition?" Professor Tobin asked quickly.

"Yes, it was a royal jewel." Lord Dacre nodded sadly. "Part of a huge necklace, but designed for a man, not a woman. It was supposed to hang down on to his chest. I found it myself. We had unearthed the most amazing tomb complex, Scruffy. Buried under an enormous pyramid, half-collapsed now. We had to dig up the entrance, and it took us a year – so many false tunnels! Traps everywhere! The ancient kings guarded their secrets well."

"And yet you still went in? Wasn't that a little unwise?" Professor Tobin looked surprised, and Maisie smiled to herself. On his own South American expedition, a few years before, the professor had almost been eaten by a huge snake! She didn't think it was very fair of him to tell Lord Dacre off.

"I couldn't *not*, Scruffy. To see the finds in their original places, that is most important. Once they are removed from the tombs and displayed in museums –" Lord Dacre waved his hand around the gallery – "they lose some of their meaning. Though we must bring them back to study, of course. I had to brave the traps and the curses to see the great king's last resting place. And when we opened the coffins – he had three of them, you know, one inside the other – the Golden Scarab was resting on his chest, above his heart."

"On his dead body!" Maisie squeaked, horrified.

"His mummy." Lord Dacre frowned at her. "Do you know nothing, child?"

"We hadn't reached the mummies, yet," Professor Tobin explained. "They're over there at the end of the room. The Egyptians preserved their dead very carefully, Maisie, then wrapped them in bandages, to keep them, er, well … not exactly fresh, but at least whole. Then they put them in these beautiful coffins. There are several mummies here in the museum."

"That's horrible," Maisie whispered. "Shouldn't they be buried?"

"Better here than sold in an Egyptian street market, young lady," Lord Dacre snapped. "For foolish tourists to buy and then bring home and unwrap at parties!" Then he seemed to relent, and he patted her hand. "Perhaps it is rather shocking, Miss Hitchins. I forget that not everyone is as fascinated with these strange death rituals as I am."

"It is fascinating, sir," Maisie gulped. "Did you say there was a curse as well?"

"Hundreds of them." Lord Dacre sighed. "Some people would probably say that the theft of the scarab was part of the curse. That it was the great king's revenge on me for robbing his resting place." He snorted. "Nonsense, of course. It was such a handsome tomb, absolutely every inch of the walls covered in paintings – and they were so lifelike, they almost seemed to move in the flickering light of our burning torches. And the furniture for the king in the afterlife – so beautifully made! There was even a carriage for him to ride in, but it was too fragile to move. I wanted everyone to see how great he was, it seemed sad that it was all hidden away. My last great work was to bring him back to life."

Maisie swallowed. She knew that Lord Dacre didn't mean that the dead king would come to life in quite that way, but it was easy to imagine, with all the talk of dark tombs and flickering torchlight. And dead bodies… Were there really bandaged-up dead people at the other end of the gallery?

"Your last great work?" Professor Tobin asked, looking at his old friend in surprise.

"My doctor has said I should not go back, Scruffy," Lord Dacre said sadly. "I have a weak heart. Too many years adventuring in the foreign sun. This was my last expedition. The scarab was my treasure. And it's gone."

Maisie had been hoping to ask Lord Dacre about her pendant – surely such an expert on Egypt would be able to tell her what the strange lines meant. After looking at the Rosetta Stone, Maisie was beginning to think that deciphering the message all by herself was going to be too tricky.

But she couldn't ask Lord Dacre for

help just now. He had his embroidered handkerchief out again, and he was blowing his nose with elephant trumpeting noises.

Mr Travers was patting him sympathetically on the back. "The police are still working on the case, my lord," he murmured. "You never know."

"I suppose so, Travers, I suppose so. Ah, well, at least there has been one pleasant part of the day, Scruffy. It has been far too long since we've met. And now that I've caught you, I'm not letting you go so easily! Won't you come and have tea with me back at Dacre House, you and Miss – Miss Hitchins, is it?"

Professor Tobin looked doubtfully at Maisie. "Would your grandmother mind?" he asked. "It's quite late..."

"I'm sure she wouldn't," Maisie said firmly, crossing her fingers behind her back.

She thought that Gran probably *would* mind – she hadn't been happy about Maisie leaving her chores to go off gallivanting with the professor in the first place. It was only Maisie reminding Gran that the museum would be educational that had persuaded her.

Luckily, Gran could be a bit of a snob, too. She would like to hear about a real lord's house, Maisie was sure. She could tell Gran that it would have been rude to refuse the invitation. Besides, she could see how eager the professor was to go and talk to his old friend, and she didn't want to drag him away.

Mr Travers hurried off to flag down a hackney large enough for four, and they all piled in. Maisie sat next to Mr Travers, with her back to the horses, so that Lord Dacre and the professor could gossip together on the journey to Chelsea.

The carriage was cold, and Maisie sat on her hands to warm them up. Mr Travers looked at her worriedly. "Would you like to borrow my scarf, Miss Hitchins?"

Maisie smiled at him. "I should think you need it more than me, being used to the hot sunshine in Egypt, sir."

"It is a shock to come back to London fog and cold," he admitted, with a shiver.

"Ah! We're almost at the house."

Mr Travers sprang out of the carriage as it drew up, helping out Lord Dacre, the professor and Maisie, and then dashing up the tall stone steps to bang the knocker on the front door.

Maisie wandered up the steps, staring admiringly at the rows and rows of glittering windows above her head. She couldn't imagine how long it would take to clean all those – or the amount of vinegar and newspaper Lord Dacre's staff would need.

The balustrades on either side of the steps were topped by statues, very like those she'd seen at the museum, lion bodies with human heads. But these were shining white marble, all the features sharp and crisp, not like the age-softened ones they'd seen that afternoon.

"Very smart sphinxes, Leggy," the professor said, patting one on the head.

Maisie could tell that he didn't really like them that much, though. He wasn't a very grand sort of person. Not like Lord Dacre, she realized, as the butler showed them into the hall. This was definitely the finest house she had ever seen. Even grander than the home of her friend Alice. There were statues and gold-painted furniture everywhere – it was like being at the museum all over again.

"Fincham, get one of the maids to fetch us some tea, please," Lord Dacre said, as he ushered them into the library – an enormous room at the back of the house. The books were impressive enough by themselves – walls full of rich, dark leather covers, the titles glinting in gold. But displayed throughout the room were Lord Dacre's most precious finds

– painted stone statues that seemed to follow Maisie with their eyes, pieces of papyrus carefully laid out under glass and even a suit of armour that Maisie was almost sure was made out of crocodile skin. It looked quite like the crocodile handbag that belonged to Miss Lane, the actress who lived on the third floor of 31 Albion Street.

The worst thing was that in the very middle of the room, there was a mummy. Lord Dacre waved them over to a little sofa, so Maisie was sitting with her back to it, and it was making her feel most uncomfortable. Mr Travers beamed at her encouragingly and handed her some tea, in the most delicate bone-china cup she'd ever seen.

"Papa!" There was a tapping of footsteps on the marble floor of the hallway, and someone called out in a high, girlish voice.

A finely dressed young woman appeared at the door, followed by a man just taking off the most absurdly tall top hat.

"Ah! Dear one. Scruffy, this is my daughter, the Honourable Isis Dacre. And my young cousin, Mr Max Dacre, who is staying with us. Isis knows a great deal about Egyptian history herself – she has been studying manuscripts since she was tiny." Lord Dacre beamed at his daughter proudly. Then he sighed. "Of course, Isis is just as devastated about the theft as I am."

Isis Dacre didn't look at all devastated, Maisie thought. In fact, as Lord Dacre turned away to introduce Max to the professor, she quite definitely rolled her eyes at her father's cousin. And Max Dacre was smiling, just a little. A slight quirk of the lips.

They didn't realize that she was watching, Maisie thought to herself, deciding that she didn't like either of them very much. As she'd entered the room Isis

Dacre's eyes had skimmed over Maisie, and noted her faded purple dress. Maisie had watched her change of expression, as she decided that this shabby little girl was of no importance.

Max Dacre didn't even seem to notice that Maisie was there at all. He really was very silly-looking, Maisie decided. He had sleeked-down black hair, and a teensy-tiny little black beard that almost looked painted on to his chin.

Maybe Isis wasn't worried because she just didn't like Egyptian history as much as her father thought she did. Maisie had a feeling that Lord Dacre might be rather hard to live with. From what she had seen of him at the museum, she suspected that he never talked about anything else, and he wasn't as good at making his stories interesting as Professor Tobin was. Maisie didn't mind when the professor talked at her while she was dusting his stuffed animals. She certainly knew more about South America than any other ten-year-old, and she was sure it would come in useful one of these days. But endless lectures about the great god Ra at the breakfast table probably wouldn't be much fun. In a house stuffed with all these ancient objects, Isis Dacre couldn't have avoided being an Egyptian scholar if she had wanted to.

"Did Mr Canning have any useful information, Papa? Have there been any other thefts?"

"No." Lord Dacre sighed. "Only my beautiful scarab. Canning has promised to keep a careful watch on the sale rooms, though, as I shall myself, of course."

Miss Dacre nodded and gave Max another strange sideways smile. Perhaps she admired him, Maisie thought, with a little shudder. Max Dacre reminded her of a snake, but Isis obviously liked him. She couldn't keep her eyes off him, and she was hardly listening to her father telling her about his visit to Mr Canning.

It seemed odd that someone who had been brought up in Lord Dacre's house, and apparently knew all about Egyptian treasures, didn't care at all that the scarab had disappeared. Even if Miss Dacre was bored with Egypt, shouldn't she be more worried about the theft itself? Someone might have broken into the house, despite what the police had said. Maisie shivered, remembering the night 31 Albion Street had been broken into, and the thief had knocked her down the stairs. She had been terrified, even as she was chasing after the thief with a frying pan. But Isis Dacre didn't seem worried about this burglary at all. She seemed much more interested in making eyes at Lord Dacre's ridiculous cousin. It really was very puzzling...

"Answer that, please, Maisie. I'm up to my elbows in dough." Gran sighed. "It's probably one of Miss Lane's admirers. Don't they know she's at the theatre getting ready by now?"

Maisie ran up the stairs to open the door, muttering to herself. She had been running around like a headless chicken, catching up on her work, ever since she'd got back from Lord Dacre's house. She was all set to tell the caller to go to the stage door, but the man standing outside didn't look like he'd come to call on Miss Lane, after all. He was short and barrel-shaped, and there were tattoos all over his hands. A sailor – he had to be.

Maisie stared at him, and he stared back. Maisie asked him who he'd come to see, noting that one of his eyes was very odd. It didn't move. And it was a completely different colour to the other eye.

"It's glass, Missy," the man said kindly. "I could see you was wondering," he added. "I lost the other to a swinging rope end, in a storm off the Cape of Good Hope. Twenty years ago, that was."

"Oh…" Maisie nodded politely. "Er, did you say who it was you'd come to visit?"

"I didn't."

Maisie couldn't think what to say. It was that eye, it seemed to keep looking at her.

"I've come to ask for a room. Card in the window says to enquire within. So here I am. Enquiring." He smiled at her, with a mouth full of blackened teeth.

"Oh! Oh, I see. Won't you step into the parlour, sir, and I'll fetch my gran from the kitchen. It's her house."

The sailor stomped into the hallway as she stood back, but he didn't go into the parlour when she held the door open. He made for the kitchen stairs instead, so that Maisie had to dash in front of him.

"I'm not much of a one for parlours," he said, grinning. "I'll go down and see your gran."

"But she's making bread," Maisie gasped. "And she doesn't like lodgers in the kitchen." How could such a plump little man wriggle his way round her so easily? He was already heading down the stairs, with Maisie somehow behind him again. Then it was too late, and he was in the kitchen, smiling his black-toothed smile at Gran and Sally.

"Good evening, Mrs Hitchins."

Maisie blinked at him – something was wrong here, she just couldn't quite put her finger on it.

"Good evening," Gran said slowly. "Maisie, you know you should show visitors into the parlour!"

"I tried!" Maisie wailed. "He wouldn't go.

The gentleman says he doesn't like parlours. He wants a room."

"I'm afraid we don't have any rooms available," Gran said briskly. "Maisie will show you back upstairs."

"Ah, now that isn't true, Mrs Hitchins. The card is in your window. You're just looking at me and not liking what you see. You see a villainous old sailor, not an honest man who's come home, tired of the nautical life."

Gran sniffed but Maisie leaned forward, staring into the seaman's wrinkled red face. She had worked it out. "I didn't tell you that she was Mrs Hitchins. I never said her name at all. How did you know?"

"Your father told me you were bright, Miss Maisie. He said he could tell from your letters."

Gran sat down suddenly with a squeak, and Sally ran to pour her a cup of water.

"You know Daniel," she murmured. "My Daniel." She turned to look over at the shawl her son had given her, which was hanging up on a hook by the door. She had told Maisie that she knew she should put it away somewhere safe, to keep it clean and fresh, but she wanted to be able to look at it for a little while first. "How is he? I've not seen him in six years. Maisie was a tiny little thing when he left."

"She looks like him." He nodded to Maisie. "You can tell Daniel Hitchins a mile off, with that flaming red hair."

"Sally, put the kettle on," Gran waved feebly at the stove. "Make tea. Excuse us, Mr – er?"

"Smith, Mrs Hitchins. Noah Smith. A good

name for a sailor, my father said. I was ship's cook aboard the *Lily Belle* these last ten years, but now I've given up the seafaring life and come home to London. So, Mrs Hitchins, might you have a room for me after all?"

Mr Smith was a decidedly odd lodger, Maisie thought, as she went out into the yard to empty her dustpan. She scurried back to the kitchen, rubbing her arms – it was freezing out there. Mr Smith didn't seem to like his rooms very much, for a start. He was hardly ever in them. He would go wandering off on great long walks around the city, and then he'd come back home and sneak down to the kitchen for a cup of tea, instead of having it properly in his own sitting room. But Gran didn't mind, for once. Mr Smith didn't seem out of place in the kitchen. Within a couple of days, she had him peeling the potatoes for dinner. Although she did come very close to sending him back upstairs when he dared to suggest a different way of seasoning her beef stew.

In fact, Mr Smith was sitting at the kitchen table right now, surrounded by newspaper. He was blacking everyone's boots, while Gran peeled vegetables for soup. Eddie was sitting on Mr Smith's feet, hoping to catch some vegetable scraps. The little dog wasn't all that keen on vegetables, but he wasn't fussy, and he'd already worked out that the old sailor was a soft touch.

The food at 31 Albion Street had definitely improved – not just because Mr Smith was helping, but because he'd paid his first month's rent as soon as he arrived without so much as a squeak. The worried look on Gran's face had eased a little, and there was a lot more meat and a lot less potato in the stew. Gran had never kept the lodgers short of food, but she and Maisie and Sally had been filling up on bread and not very much butter for a while.

The bell rang, and as Maisie hurried back into the kitchen, Mr Smith nodded at it jingling away on the wall.

"That's the professor, ain't it?" he asked, as Maisie rinsed her dirty hands. "Probably wanting tea for his smart company. Hope he's covered up that bird of his. Parrots – you never know what they might say."

"Oh, I don't think Jasper's rude," Maisie said, smiling. "He's not a very clever parrot. He hardly ever says anything except 'Polly want a cracker'. Most of the time he just squawks and hangs upside down in his cage. Has the professor got company, then? Sally must have let them in while I was out running errands."

Mr Smith liked the professor – they had spent a whole afternoon discussing the South

Sea Islands, and whether or not sea serpents were real. Maisie thought Professor Tobin was a good judge of character, so she was glad to see them getting on. She knew deep down that Mr Smith couldn't be as villainous as he looked, especially as Eddie liked him, too, but his strange blue glass eye still made her feel odd. As though the old sailor could look inside her head, and see what she was thinking. She knew that was silly, but she couldn't help worrying about it.

Although actually, she decided, as she ran up the stairs to Professor Tobin's rooms, it would be very useful for a detective to have an eye that could do that. She was still wondering about the missing scarab, and Miss Dacre and her strange sideways looks. If only she could just see what people were thinking!

"You rang, Professor?" she asked. "Oh!

Good morning, Lord Dacre," she added, bobbing a curtsey as she realized who the professor's company was. Lord Dacre was sitting in the armchair across from the professor's and he looked distinctly miserable.

"Did you want tea, Professor?"

"Yes and no, Maisie." Professor Tobin beckoned her in. "A cup of tea would cheer his lordship up, I'm sure, but I also wanted you to see this." He pointed to the little table in between them, and Maisie gasped. "You found it!"

Lying on top of the professor's newspaper was a huge golden ornament, the size of Maisie's hand. It was clearly a beetle. It reminded her of the black beetles they sometimes found in the scullery copper, the great iron tub where they heated the hot water for washing. Maisie always had to chase them out before they began the weekly wash, as they gave Gran the collywobbles. She didn't like their scrabbly little legs. But this beetle was fat and glossy, made of something smooth and blue which glowed so richly that Maisie could hardly believe

the jewel was
thousands of
years old.
It had wings,
great curved golden 
and blue ones, and it was holding the sun
in its claws – a ball of glowing amber.

Maisie looked at Lord Dacre in
confusion. If the scarab had been
recovered, why did he look so unhappy?
"Did you have to pay a reward to get it
back, my lord?" she asked.

"What?" Lord Dacre seemed to be sunk
deep in thought. He looked up at her and
blinked vaguely. "Oh… Tea. Please."

Professor Tobin sighed and nodded to
Maisie. "Fetch it for us, would you, Maisie,
and I will explain when you get back."

Maisie dashed back downstairs to tell

Gran about their visitor and to make the tea. She muttered crossly at the kettle as it took an age to boil. There was clearly something mysterious going on – perhaps even something more interesting than the theft itself. Lord Dacre definitely didn't look like someone who was delighted to have his precious treasure returned.

"Are you sure he's a lord, Maisie?" Gran muttered, hurrying about. "Goodness gracious. You'd better use the best tea. And take some biscuits!"

"He didn't look like he wanted biscuits, Gran, he's ever so gloomy. I shouldn't think he'll even notice. But I'll take them. And, yes, I've already got the silver teapot."

"Don't be cheeky, Maisie," her gran murmured, but she didn't sound as though she really meant it. She was far too worried about entertaining a lord. "And for heaven's sake, don't spill tea on him!"

Maisie escaped back upstairs carrying the tray, with Gran still calling after her about remembering to use the sugar tongs, and not to speak unless she was spoken to. Lord Dacre brightened up very slightly when he saw the tea tray, but as he moved the scarab out of the way for her to put the tray down and laid it on his lap, he let out the most enormous sigh.

Maisie raised her eyebrows at Professor Tobin. What was wrong with Lord Dacre now? "He's got it back!" she whispered. "What's the matter?"

"Pour the tea, Maisie. Leggy, tell Maisie what's happened."

"Tell the maid?" Lord Dacre looked at her, vaguely surprised. "Wait a moment, isn't this the young lady who was with you at the museum?"

"Miss Hitchins is a detective, Leggy. She's most experienced. She solved a series of daring art thefts recently, and helped to capture the infamous Sparrow Gang. You might have read about the case in the newspaper." Professor Tobin beamed encouragingly at Maisie. "She is also my landlady's granddaughter and, yes, she works as a housemaid. I took her to the museum to learn more about Egypt. She is, er, naturally curious."

He was trying to find a polite way to say that she was downright nosy, Maisie decided, but she didn't mind.

"I really don't think..." Lord Dacre began, looking at Maisie doubtfully. "And I don't have that long, Scruffy. I need to get back to St Katharine Docks. There's another ship come in, you know, with more of my artefacts from the tomb. I need to oversee the unloading – no one understands how delicate those finds are!"

"Miss Hitchins has been consulted by the police, Leggy. They know of her at Scotland Yard!"

Maisie tried not to smirk. They certainly did. Inspector Fred Grange had been one of Gran's lodgers and he knew Maisie quite well. In fact, he'd probably tell Lord Dacre that she was a meddling little so-and-so. But he would have to admit that it was Maisie's detective work that had led to the capture of Charlie Sparrow.

"She's a little girl!"

"Exactly, my lord," Maisie said briskly. "It's ever such a good disguise for a detective. No one ever suspects. Now, why are you looking so downright miserable when you've got your beetle back? Did you have to pay a huge reward?"

Lord Dacre flinched when he heard her refer to his precious scarab as a beetle, but Maisie didn't feel like being all that polite.

"No. No reward. It was found. But it isn't complete," he said, glaring at her.

"Oh..." Maisie peered at it. "May I see, my lord?"

He held it out, cradling it lovingly in his hands, and Maisie saw at last what was wrong. The glowing blue of the body and the fiery amber sun had been so beautiful that she hadn't realized. The beetle's head was solid gold, as far as she could tell, but there were two round holes where its eyes should be. Someone had gouged them out. She could even see faint scratches around the eye sockets where it had been clumsily done.

"The eyes are missing," she said. "Someone took them and left the rest?"

"Curious, isn't it?" the professor agreed. "How much is this treasure worth, Leggy? All this gold and precious enamelwork?"

"Thousands of pounds, I suppose," Lord Dacre murmured. "It must be, but it's hard to say. No one has ever sold anything like it. I don't want to sell it!"

The professor turned to Maisie. "It had ruby eyes, you see. Two quite large rubies. Very valuable in themselves, of course, but much more precious as part of the scarab. Someone has taken the rubies and just thrown the rest away."

"Oh!" Maisie looked up from the scarab in surprise. "I thought the police must have found it and brought it back. Was it really thrown away?"

"A gang of mudlarks found it early this morning at low tide, buried in the muddy bank of the Thames," Lord Dacre told her. "Someone pulled out the eyes, and then threw my scarab in the river!" He cupped his hands around it, as though he wanted to keep it safe. "The boys took it to a pawnbroker, who had the sense to see that this was nothing like the cheap necklaces and brass rings he usually deals with. He paid them something for their trouble, and then he went to the museum to show them what he'd found. Mr Canning sent for me straight away."

"And the eyes are gone..." Maisie said thoughtfully. "I suppose the thief kept those. Although if they were thrown in the river, too, there's no telling where they might have ended up. Why would anyone do that? Is the scarab too unusual to sell, my lord?"

"Probably," Lord Dacre admitted. "To sell it for its real value, the thieves would need to take the scarab to an expert – and any expert would know who it belongs to. I have given private lectures, you see, since I returned with my treasures. The scarab is well known among Egyptian scholars. It was to feature in my book," he added sadly. "A very talented artist has made several sketches of it."

"But why throw away the golden part?" Maisie frowned. "They could have melted it down, even if they couldn't sell it as it is..."

Lord Dacre let out a strangled sort of yelp and clutched at his chest, his eyes bulging painfully. "Melted it down!" he gasped. "Oh, my heart… My precious scarab…"

Maisie hastily poured him a cup of tea. "I'm so sorry, my lord, I was just thinking aloud. Please don't take on so. They didn't, did they? It's here, look…" She glanced worriedly at the professor. She hadn't realized quite how upset his lordship was.

"Tell her the rest, Leggy," Professor Tobin said firmly. "And do calm down."

"There's more, then." Maisie sat down on the floor next to Professor Tobin's chair and pulled her little notebook out of her apron pocket.

Lord Dacre took several deep, shaky breaths, and then nodded. "More, yes. Did I mention curses, when we met at the museum? Curses supposed to have been left by the pharaohs on their tombs? All nonsense, of course," he added, but this time he didn't sound so sure.

"You're worried you're under a curse?" Maisie said sympathetically. After his lordship's description of the shadowy tomb, and the paintings that seemed to move in the torchlight, she wasn't surprised that he was jumpy.

"No, no… Well…" He heaved a huge sigh. "Only in my darkest moments, anyway. But Isis is convinced that the pharaoh is taking his revenge. She's frightened that the scarab being discovered without its eyes is the most terrible threat! She's even started talking the most ridiculous gibberish about secret societies carrying on through the centuries to bring about the pharaoh's curse, if his tomb should be discovered!"

Maisie blinked. "I'm not sure that I understand…"

"Me neither," Professor Tobin muttered.

"Some sort of gang. The great-great-great-however-many-times-grandsons of the pharaoh's servants. Summoned to attack the thief – that's me – and defend their master's honour!" Lord Dacre stared at them both, his watery blue eyes bulging worriedly.

"That's just silly," Maisie said, after a moment's disbelieving silence.

"Oh, I know," Lord Dacre agreed. "But after listening to my daughter having hysterics for three hours this morning, even I almost believed it. And you have to admit, the removal of the eyes – it is rather, um, *unpleasant*. One could read all sorts of nasty meanings into it. And believe me, my daughter has. She has retired to bed, she worked herself into a nervous collapse."

Maisie had to hold back a sniff. It would be nice to be rich enough to have a day to waste on a nervous collapse, she thought. Perhaps *she* could have one next washday.

"Poor little Isis," Professor Tobin said, giving Maisie a sly sideways glance.

"Indeed." Lord Dacre heaved another enormous sigh. "And she and Max were meant to be helping me check over the unloaded finds from the ship again, too. Most inconvenient. Anyway, it is all the more important to find out what is going on," Lord Dacre said firmly. "I need to convince my daughter that I am completely safe and all this talk of curses is just ridiculous. And of course I must find the rubies – the scarab loses so much of its character without them. Not to mention its value." He eyed Maisie doubtfully. "Scruffy assures me that you are a brilliant detective, Miss Hitchins. And I must say, the housemaid disguise is very good."

Maisie opened her mouth to explain that it wasn't really a disguise – Lord Dacre didn't seem to understand that she actually did work in the boarding house. Perhaps he didn't think of servants as people who could think for themselves? But then she caught Professor Tobin's eye, and saw that he was shaking his head very slightly. He was right. It was easier to let Lord Dacre think what he wanted – especially as it was the most interesting case, and she didn't want his lordship to decide she wasn't up to it. She simply smiled at him and nodded.

Lord Dacre held out the golden beetle, blind and broken, and stared at her hopefully. "Will you help me, Miss Hitchins?"

Maisie shivered and huddled the checked muffler tighter around her shoulders. It had snowed in the night, and Gran had fussed over her before she went out to the grocer, telling her to go and put on a flannel petticoat and thick woollen stockings. She looked up thoughtfully at the greyish, heavy-looking sky. Would it snow again? And how soon? At least her basket wasn't all that heavy – it held just a few bits of shopping that Gran had needed, biscuits and such. But it was a terribly long way down to the River Thames, too far to walk in the snow. Too far to walk without taking so long that Gran would send out a search party, anyway. And she had to make sure she was there at low tide, while the mudlarks were out hunting for scraps along the muddy bank.

She had asked Mr Smith about the way the river's tides worked, but she hadn't been able to ask about exact times, as he'd given her a very suspicious look. "You ain't going down there, are you, Maisie? That's not a place for a nice girl like you." It was lucky that George the butcher's boy had turned up with the meat delivery just at the right time, and given Maisie an excuse to hurry away.

She was planning to go and see where the scarab had been found. She had got up that morning determined to find some time for her investigations, and nipping out to the shops seemed like a perfect excuse. But now it was dreadfully cold, and she was ever so tempted to hurry back to the warmth of the kitchen at Albion Street. Her boots were damp and her feet ached. Eddie looked up at her hopefully. His ears were drooping and he kept lifting up his paws and putting them down again, as if he hoped the snow might have gone away in between.

Gran had given Maisie threepence that very morning. She had said she knew that Maisie missed being able to buy sweets and that, as she was going to the grocers, she might as well take the chance to get some. Maisie had been tempted, looking at the glass jars – she had fancied some liquorice, or perhaps bulls' eyes, since they lasted such a long time. But she hadn't taken her own little purse out of her coat pocket, in the end, so she was still quite rich. She had two shillings from Lord Dacre, as well, for what he called "expenses". Maisie smiled to herself as she waited at the corner of the road for the horse-drawn omnibus. Horse buses weren't very grand, but it would be much, much warmer than walking.

Lord Dacre had told her that the scarab had been picked up by a gang of boys mudlarking – it must have been a surprising find for them, Maisie thought. She didn't know anyone who'd ever made a living that way, though she had seen them at it when she'd walked over the bridges. Mudlarks were scavengers who sold things that washed up at the edge of the river – firewood, lumps of coal, copper nails, whatever they could find. Not golden beetles, usually.

Maisie had envied them sometimes, on the hottest of days, when they were wading about in the water and she was buttoned into layers of petticoats. But she had been shocked to hear that there were boys out on the riverbanks now, scavenging in weather like this. It had been freezing cold yesterday, when the scarab had been found, even if it hadn't yet snowed. Did they still go picking through the mud in the depths of winter? Wouldn't it all be frozen, anyway?

She waved wildly to the omnibus as it came rattling down the street, paid the conductor and climbed aboard, wrinkling her nose at the wet, muddy straw all over the floor. Still, she was about to go down to the Thames and pick her way over the riverbank, which was nothing but mud with some rubbish thrown in. That would be much worse than a bit of muddy straw.

Maisie sat down next to a thin, elderly lady who peered at her disapprovingly over pince-nez spectacles. "Good morning," Maisie murmured politely.

"Please make sure not to tread on my feet!" the elderly lady snapped, as the omnibus swung wildly round a corner. "And keep that dog under control!"

Maisie pulled her feet the other way as far as she could and picked up Eddie, holding him tightly, but the old lady simply gave a disgusted sniff. Maisie gave up trying to be polite and just stared out of the dirty window, trying to see if it was going to snow again. It was awfully slow, this journey, she thought worriedly. Perhaps on the way back she had better go by the Underground. She had said to Gran that she had errands to run for Professor Tobin as well. Hopefully that would stop Gran worrying where she had got to.

Maisie still had a little way to walk when she got off the omnibus. Lord Dacre had explained to her that the boys were known to work down towards Wapping and the docks. He had told her to ask the way to the Pelican Stairs, down to the river. It was not a part of the city that Maisie had ever been to before. She hurried along the alleyway that a young man pointed out to her, wishing she had never come. In the grey winter cold, with the snow already turning to filthy slush, the streets were eerily empty – but at the same time she felt as though she was being watched.

Maisie hesitated at the top of the stone steps. They were caked in mud and slime, and she couldn't help thinking of the sewers, pouring out who knew what into the river. She frowned. If there was mud and weedy slime up the stairs like this, then that must mean the water came all the way up, too.

At that moment the river seemed a long way away, sucking sullenly at the mud. She knew that the river moved with the tides here, being quite close to the sea, but surely it didn't move as much as that? Could it truly rise all the way up a flight of stairs?

"What you want?" someone asked.

Maisie jumped and almost slipped on the worn stairway. She dug her nails into the damp wall down the side of the steps, gasping in fright.

"What you standing there like that for?" the boy demanded again. At least, Maisie thought it was a boy. He was so filthy with mud that it was hard to tell, but the face under his dirty cap looked quite young. He was wearing ragged trousers that were tucked up to show bare legs, scarlet with cold, and a pair of boots tied on with scraps of knotted string. There was a metal bucket dangling on his arm, full of holes.

"I'm looking for the boys that found the scarab – the golden beetle that was in the river yesterday." Maisie eyed him doubtfully. "At least, I was told it was a gang of boys that found it. Were you there?" She shuddered as she watched his thin, dirty face. Maisie had been feeling hard done by on three meals a day, but these children were surviving on the few pence they could earn for selling other people's rubbish.

"Don't know about that," the boy said at once, but his eyes slipped shiftily sideways, and Maisie didn't believe him. She glanced over, trying to see where the boy was looking, and saw a few more children, stooping over closer to the water, gathering scraps into tattered baskets.

"Was it them?" Maisie asked. "I'm not here to get anyone into trouble," she added quickly. "I just wondered if you could tell me where it was thrown in. Whether the tide always brings things the same way?" She shifted nervously on the steps. The other children had seen her now and they were creeping closer.

Eddie peered round Maisie's skirts and let out a low, uncertain growl. Maisie swallowed, and wondered if she should just turn and run. But why would they want to threaten her?

"Who's she?" a grey-faced girl demanded. "Why you talking to her?"

"Standing there snooping, wasn't she?" the first boy snapped back.

"This is our patch," snarled a tiny boy in a longcoat, with black rat tails of greasy hair trailing down his back. "Get your own."

"Don't be stupid," the older boy told him, rolling his eyes. "Look at her! She's not coming down here to pick up coal, is she? She's a nark."

"I am not!" Maisie said indignantly. She knew that slang from her friend George. A nark was a nose – someone who went sniffing around for the police. Well, maybe she was. But not in the way this lot meant it.

"I'm not working for the police," Maisie insisted. "I'm working for the man who lost that golden beetle. Trying to find who stole it from him in the first place. His family are really worried, they think it might be…" Maisie trailed off. How could she explain Egyptian kings and ancient curses to these starved children? Especially when she could hardly make sense of it herself. "They think someone's after him," she said, shrugging.

"I only wanted to know where it might have gone in, that was all."

They all looked at her suspiciously for a minute longer, and then the boy seemed to relax a little. He shifted the bucket further up his arm. "It was me what found it," he admitted.

"But we dunno where it went in," the weary-looking girl told Maisie. "Can't tell. Most stuff just falls off the ships. And it all depends on the rain."

"I suppose it would," Maisie agreed.

"It din't fall off no ship," the boy in the huge coat squeaked.

"Shut up, Greasy," the weary girl said disgustedly. "You don't know nothing."

"I do, too! I saw him, din't I?"

There was a moment of stillness, as everyone turned to stare at the tiny boy.

"Saw who?" Maisie asked.

"Some swell. He threw it in off the bridge. I was up there – I saw it go. Late afternoon, it was. Almost dark. Saw it sparklin', an' I tried to catch it, but it went in the water. Then *he* nicked it off me." He heaved his elbow at the older boy, who snorted.

"That's right, Greasy, it were yours an' I nicked it – the next morning. Who you trying to kid? You din't see no swell. An' even if you did, it could've been anything he threw off the bridge."

"That would be Tower Bridge?" Maisie asked, trying to work out where they were. The new bridge was the closest one, she was sure. Tower Bridge opened up in the middle so the tall-masted ships could sail through to the docks.

The little boy nodded. "He did throw it," he muttered, glaring at the others. "And he *were* a swell, Lily Dickens. He had a great tall hat on, so there!"

Maisie wasn't sure she believed the little boy, either – perhaps he was just making it all up in the hope of a reward?

"Did you get paid much?" she asked the older boy suddenly. "For the scarab, I mean? You took it to a pawnbroker, didn't you?"

"Five shillings." The boy shook his head in amazement. "Gave it to my ma, paid all the rent. Best haul ever."

Maisie swallowed and nodded. Five shillings. According to Lord Dacre, the scarab was worth thousands of pounds. And the boy thought he had been well rewarded, even though he was back here the next day, searching through mud and ice for firewood to sell.

She looked around her at their pale, pinched faces and the purplish red of their bare legs, and shivered. She pulled the bag of biscuits out of her basket and handed it to the boy, since he seemed to be in charge. She could use some of the money from Lord Dacre to buy another bag for Gran.

"Thank you for talking to me," she said quietly, turning to walk back up the steps.

At the top, she glanced back, but none of them were looking at her at all – they were desperately shaking the last few crumbs out of the bag.

Maisie was walking back to Albion Street, after her second trip to the grocer's – trying to work out how to explain to Gran that she had been away for the whole morning, even though she'd taken the Underground back – when she came to a sudden stop. Something the little boy said had suddenly clicked inside her head.

A smartly dressed man – no ordinary burglar, then, not if he was wearing a top hat. In fact, she should have worked that out already. It couldn't be just any old thief, breaking in on the off-chance. That house was so full of gold, they'd never have left with only the scarab. The thief had known just what to take. Exactly what would upset Lord Dacre the most.

Perhaps the police were right – it almost had to be an inside job…

Eddie gave a whine, and Maisie realized the little dog was shivering. There were a few flakes of snow starting to feather down around them. "Sorry," she whispered to him. "I know it's too cold to stop and think." Maisie set off again, hurrying home. There was an odd smell in the air, something like the smell of the fireplace grates, but mixed with the cold sharpness of the snow. Then she saw that the dense greyness of the sky wasn't just the snow clouds – it was smoke. Something was burning.

Maisie was close enough to home to feel

a sudden coldness inside, as well as out. What if Professor Tobin had piled up the coals and set the hearthrug on fire? Or Miss Lane had knocked a candle over on to one of her lacy scarves? But the fire was in the next street, she realized, the thud of her heart slowing down. Flames were flickering in an upstairs window, and there was a horrible, hungry crackling sound. People spilled out on to the steps, clutching children and frantically calling to each other, trying to make sure that no one had been left behind.

"Bring the teaspoons! The silver teaspoons!" one elderly lady screamed to her husband, who was struggling to carry a very large and ugly portrait of a man with side whiskers. The old lady herself had a huge and terrified ginger cat tucked under her arm.

Maisie reached down to catch Eddie's collar, just in case, but the little dog seemed to know that this was not the time for chasing cats. Maisie wondered if she ought to stop and help, or perhaps run to the post office and telegraph the fire station, but the engine from the Metropolitan Fire Brigade was already swinging around the corner, drawn by two sweating horses. A gang of small boys standing watching the flames let out a huge cheer as the engine drew up. The bell was clanging so loudly that Eddie tucked himself in between Maisie's feet, whimpering. Maisie hurried him out of the way as the firemen jumped off the engine and started to fit the hose to the steam pump.

Maisie walked on home, turning back to look every so often, and worrying about those people, out in the cold with only the strange treasures they had snatched up as they'd fled from the fire.

"I'd take you," she whispered to Eddie. "And Gran, of course. And Sally and all the lodgers. I don't know what else I'd take – my most precious things… Oh! My magnifying glass. And my notebook." She sighed. Even the poor people from the burning house still had more than the mudlarks.

"Maisie! Maisie!"

Maisie galloped up the stairs, wondering what on earth was the matter with the professor. She had taken up his letters, and now he was ringing his bell and shouting for her so loudly that Gran had nearly dropped the teapot.

"Whatever is it?" Maisie gasped, as she

reached the landing.

The professor hauled her into his sitting room and pressed a letter into her hands. "Read that! Yes, this bit, here. It's from Leggy."

Maisie frowned at the loopy, flourishing handwriting and felt glad that it was only a short note. "Someone's painting messages up in hieroglyphics?" she asked, hoping she'd read it right.

"The first one appeared a couple of nights ago, apparently. On the wall opposite Leggy's house. And then another last night, on the wall of his club, the Explorers. Miss Dacre has had another nervous attack."

"Does Lord Dacre knows what they mean, these messages? Is it something horrible, is that why his daughter's so upset?" Maisie said, trying to read the rest of the note, but the writing only got worse. Even though Lord Dacre wrote that he wasn't worried, Maisie had a feeling he was putting on a brave face, and these new threats had shaken him even more.

"Apparently they're all about death..." Professor Tobin sighed worriedly. "I have to admit, Maisie, I'm starting to find this rather frightening."

Maisie smoothed the letter between her fingers, looking at the words straggling across the page.

"Yes. But there's one odd thing, Professor..." She nibbled her bottom lip, thinking it through. "It's the same thing that I thought about the scarab, actually..."

"Oh, do tell me!" Professor Tobin begged impatiently.

"Don't you think it's strange that no one

has asked for anything?" Maisie nodded slowly. "Whoever took the scarab could have ransomed it for a lot of money – it's obvious that Lord Dacre would have paid anything to get it back. Instead they just pulled out its eyes and threw it away. They didn't even mean for it to be found. That was an accident, I think. After all, they threw it into the river! And now with these messages. They're just being nasty. They aren't telling Lord Dacre to pay money, or give back the finds, or anything."

The professor sighed gustily, making his moustache flap. "Well, isn't that the point? They're just frightening him."

"But why?" Maisie shrugged. "It seems to be an awful lot of trouble for nothing. Oh!" She sat down suddenly on the very edge of an armchair, looking pale.

“Have some of my tea, Maisie,” the professor said anxiously, holding out a cup. “What is it? Have you thought of something?”

Maisie nodded miserably. “Lord Dacre told us it was his last expedition, because of his heart trouble. What if someone is trying to frighten him to death?”

"Please, George..." Maisie begged. "It'll take forever to do it all by myself. And Gran says she'll pay you sixpence."

"Oh, all right, then." George grinned at her and leaned his bicycle against the railings. "I've only got a couple of deliveries left to make, and Mr Harrowby won't know, I suppose. I'll just tell him the snow slowed me down. Got a shovel?"

Maisie handed him the shovel from the outhouse, and went back to sweeping the snow off the front steps. There had been a heavy snowfall in the night, and the steps and the street in front of the house were ankle deep. They had to be clear for the lodgers to go up and down. Gran had given her a bag of salt to scatter on the steps to stop them freezing over.

"What's the matter?" George asked, a few minutes later, leaning on his shovel, scarlet-cheeked.

Maisie stared at him. "Nothing. What do you mean?"

"Got to be something wrong, Maisie, you ain't chatting."

"Oh…" Maisie nodded. "I suppose so. It's this case. I don't know what to do next."

"You got another one?" George asked curiously. He had been part of the very first mystery that Maisie had solved, when he'd been accused of stealing from the butcher's where he worked. He'd had a particular interest in her detecting ever since, and had helped her out on a couple of her other cases.

"Lord Dacre's scarab. It's been in the papers," Maisie said proudly.

"You're mixed up in that?" George's eyes widened. "Maisie, the newspapers are saying there's a curse on that golden beetle thing!"

"Curses are nonsense," Maisie said firmly. Out here, with the weak winter sun shining on the snow, she believed that. It was harder to be so certain when it was dark. "I think it was somebody from his house. Somebody who knew how much it would upset him if that beetle was taken. His lordship's got a weak heart..."

"You think someone's trying to do away with him?" George asked.

"Maybe. But I've got no proof," Maisie admitted. "I'm just guessing."

"Who's your suspect, then?"

Maisie sighed. "His daughter... And his cousin, I think."

George stared at her. "Why?"

Maisie shrugged a little. She couldn't just say that it was because she didn't like them. That wasn't proper detecting, it was stupid.

"They've got the opportunity," she murmured, not looking at George.

"Well, you need more than that," he scoffed.

"I know!" Maisie snapped back. "But the police think it was an inside job, too."

George sniffed, as though he didn't think much of that, either, and Maisie sighed and shivered.

"Anyway, I'm working on it. Come on, cleverclogs. Gran wants this all cleared by lunchtime."

Maisie sat curled up in bed, with Eddie snoring slightly on the rug beside her. She was making a list of clues and possible suspects in her notebook, and it was not going very well. Most of her notes were crossed out, and her pencil needed sharpening.

She blew out her candle with a huffy little sigh and lay down, trying to think the case through. It was too cold for sitting up in bed writing anyway. Gran had left the stove banked up with coals to keep the warmth in, but Maisie was frozen, even with Gran's old quilted bedjacket on over her nightgown.

"Eddie!" Maisie whispered, hoping he wasn't too deeply asleep. "Eddie!"

The little dog looked up blearily and wagged his tail.

"Come on up. Come on. I know you aren't supposed to, but my feet are freezing, and you must be perishing, too. Good boy!" She patted her feet, and Eddie sprang up delightedly on to the bed. "Oh, that's better," she murmured, as Eddie settled himself snugly on her toes.

"How am I going to find any evidence to show Lord Dacre, Eddie?" Maisie asked sleepily. "I can't say I think it was Isis or Max unless I've got some real proof, and how am I ever going to get that? I'd have to interview them, and why would they talk to me? I wonder if we could go to the house..." She yawned, and Eddie sniffed and wriggled himself into a tighter little ball on top of her feet. "I wonder where those rubies have got to..." Maisie mumbled to herself, as she drifted off to sleep.

"Look, Maisie, this is about Lord Dacre. Isn't that the professor's friend? That lord who came to the house?" Gran asked, pointing at the newspaper, which was spread out across the kitchen table.

Maisie hid a grin. Gran knew perfectly well who Lord Dacre was. She just liked to mention that a lord had visited as often as she could, especially as Mr Smith was sitting at the table, sipping – or rather slurping – his morning cup of tea.

"What does it say about him?" Maisie asked.

Gran squinted at the tiny print. "Major developments. Case solved, apparently."

"They've got the thief? Who is it?" Maisie squeaked. "Who's been arrested? When Lord Dacre came to visit a couple of days ago, he was talking about an Egyptian secret society!"

Mr Smith snorted. "Lot of nonsense!"

"Yes, well, I think Lord Dacre thought so, too." Maisie replied. "But I didn't know that there were even any suspects."

"Well, Inspector Grange— Oh, our old

lodger!" Gran glanced smugly at Mr Smith. "It says he's arrested an Algernon Travers."

"Mr Travers?" Maisie gaped at her. "Lord Dacre's nice secretary? But – I met him..."

"That doesn't mean he can't be a thief, Maisie!" Gran laughed.

"I know, but..." Maisie frowned. Mr Travers? Really? He had seemed so kind, and he'd been polite to her and the professor. Surely he couldn't be a thief.

"Gran, can I pop out this afternoon? Please? Just for a very short while. I think I ought to pay a visit to Scotland Yard and congratulate Inspector Grange on his promotion..."

"Good afternoon, Inspector." Maisie bobbed a polite curtsey, but she was smiling, and Inspector Fred Grange beamed back at her. When they'd first met, he'd been calling himself Mr Grange and masquerading as a clerk at the biscuit factory. He'd been the last person to rent the second-floor rooms, before Mr Smith had arrived. Maisie had noticed Mr Grange hanging around the streets when he should have been at work, and had asked him some very careful questions, which anyone who knew anything about biscuits should have been able to answer. It had been very good detective work.

Unfortunately, she had then assumed that he was an international art thief, instead of an undercover policeman, but anyone could have made that mistake. After Maisie had helped Sergeant Grange to break the art thieves' secret codes, he had been promoted to Inspector.

"Like the new office?" he asked proudly.

Maisie nodded, and tactfully didn't point out that his office was narrower than the broom cupboard at Albion Street.

"Very nice! And we read about you in the newspaper this morning."

Inspector Grange shrugged modestly. "Oh, they write a lot of humbug. It was a simple case. No need to make all that fuss." But he was smiling to himself. "It had to be someone knowledgeable about ancient Egypt, you see. To paint all those strange messages. There weren't that many suspects."

Maisie gave a tiny sigh. "Are you absolutely sure you've got the right person?" she asked. She didn't want to spoil Inspector Grange's case, but she was convinced that he had the wrong man.

"Of course I am!" Inspector Grange glared at her. "Maisie Hitchins, don't tell me that you've got inside information about this case as well!"

"Lord Dacre is a friend of the professor's," Maisie admitted. "And I've met Mr Travers. He's so nice!"

"Lots of criminals are very charming," the inspector snapped.

"Oh, I know, it's just that..." Maisie shook her head. "It doesn't feel right. He loved the Egyptian exhibits in the museum so much. He took me all round and told me about them, while Professor Tobin chatted to Lord Dacre. And the way he talked about them was so ... so *respectful*, I can't imagine him pulling the eyes out of the scarab, or throwing it into the river. He just wouldn't do that." She looked worriedly at Inspector Grange. "Poor Mr Travers. Are you really sure? You've got evidence?"

"Well, he hasn't actually confessed. And we didn't find the missing rubies in his rooms... But of course we have evidence, Maisie! Scotland Yard doesn't make mistakes about that sort of thing," Inspector Grange said irritably.

Maisie thought that he looked the tiniest bit worried, and he hustled her out of his office quite soon after. She wondered if she ought to tell him about the man in the tall hat that the little mudlark had seen – she couldn't imagine Mr Travers in a silly hat like that. But that was just her feeling – and Inspector Grange didn't seem to be in a mood to listen.

Knowing that Mr Travers had been arrested had suddenly made everything much more urgent. Maisie couldn't bear to think of him shut up in a cell. But Inspector Grange was right – there just weren't that many people who could have painted those hieroglyphic messages. It made sense that the burglary was an inside job – and Mr Travers was an obvious suspect, even if Maisie couldn't think why he would have done it.

"Maybe I was wrong about him..." she muttered to herself, slowly climbing the stairs to the first floor. Her feet felt heavy. "I thought he was such a lovely man. But then, I suppose I did think Inspector Grange was an art thief, once." She sighed. "I don't want to believe it. That's the problem. I'll just have to try harder to find some evidence one way or the other," she added, as she knocked on Professor Tobin's door. She needed to find out more about the theft. Perhaps she could prove that it hadn't been Mr Travers, somehow? That surely had to be easier than finding out who it *had* been...

"Travers?" Professor Tobin said disbelievingly, when she told him the news. "Nonsense! A very sound chap, I thought.

Sensible, and a first-class brain."

Maisie tried not to grin. It was lucky that Mr Travers had admired the professor's work.

"I know," she agreed. "I thought so, too. And he was so kind, showing me round the gallery. I don't see why he'd do it! He liked Lord Dacre, I could tell, and he loved his job. He was as enthusiastic about the finds as Lord Dacre was. What good could it possibly do him to steal the scarab and then terrify his own employer?"

"But the police must have thought of that, Maisie..." Professor Tobin frowned. "They can't have arrested him for no reason at all."

"They must have some sort of evidence," Maisie agreed. "But I'm not sure Inspector Grange was happy with it. He wouldn't tell me why they'd arrested Mr Travers." She looked at him hopefully. "Professor, I don't suppose you feel like visiting Dacre House, do you? I thought that if I could look at the scene of the crime I might find some answers. And it would be ever so much easier if you came with me. I know you asked Lord Dacre to let me investigate, but I'm not sure he really believes I can help. I've a feeling that the servants might just send me away. Especially as Lord Dacre is so upset by everything that's going on."

Professor Tobin nodded. "We'll go at once, Maisie. Run and fetch your coat, and then see if you can find a cab." He bustled about, finding a pair of stout boots and a thick overcoat with a fur collar, and Maisie hurried to find her own warmest things and explain to Gran that the professor had asked her to go with him.

"Off on another educational visit, Maisie?" Gran asked her grimly. "Like the museum?"

"We're going to Lord Dacre's, Gran," Maisie explained. "It'll be very educational – full of Egyptian artefacts." *And thieves*, she felt like adding. *I'm sure the thief is someone from the house, but not Mr Travers.*

"Oh, very well," Gran murmured, impressed in spite of herself by Maisie visiting such a grand house again. "Behave! Don't do anything unladylike!"

Maisie smiled. "I promise!" But she had her fingers crossed behind her back. Sometimes, detectives just had to be a little bit unladylike. If not downright deceitful. Maisie didn't really like telling lies, but sometimes there was nothing else she could do.

"What are they doing?" Maisie murmured to the professor, as they got out of the cab. Two of Lord Dacre's footmen were perched on those strange statues outside the house with buckets and cloths, scrubbing at the marble.

"They look like they're riding on them." Maisie tried not to giggle. But then she frowned as she noticed the red marks on the stone. "Oh, what if someone's left another message?"

One of the footman clambered off the back of his sphinx and grumpily showed them into the house. Fincham the butler came hurrying to meet them, looking harassed.

"Good morning, Professor. Yes, yes of course. His lordship is in the library." He trotted across the hall, beckoning them after him, and Maisie watched in surprise. When she had visited before, the butler had been so grand – he had seemed to glide everywhere instead of walking. Something had clearly upset him very much.

"I still can't believe it," Lord Dacre said sadly, as he came to shake the professor's hand. "Travers! The police seem so sure. Oh, do sit down. Fincham will bring tea." He waved them over to a sofa. "Yes, Travers is the last person I would have expected to betray me in such a dreadful fashion."

"Exactly," Maisie muttered.

"But Max saw him, you know," Lord Dacre

explained, shaking his head. "Poor chap didn't say so at once. Said he didn't want to believe it himself. He liked Travers, too! Besides, who was he to know why Travers was sneaking around in the middle of the night, he said. He thought perhaps Travers and I were working late. But then when the scarab was found so badly damaged, and the messages began to appear, Max decided he had to say something."

Maisie glanced sideways at the professor. It all sounded very fishy to her. Surely in a police investigation, no one would be stupid enough to hold back that sort of evidence? Perhaps Mr Max Dacre just wanted to throw the police off the scent, Maisie thought. Inspector Grange had told her that the police were sure it was an inside job – and Max Dacre was inside, too…

"And then dear Isis admitted to me that Travers had been behaving very strangely," Lord Dacre went on, with a huge sigh. "He wrote her a poem, apparently, and he kept picking flowers for her in the garden. She was forced to tell him that it must stop. She thinks maybe he stole the scarab because she made him angry."

Maisie blinked. She hadn't seen any signs of Mr Travers mooning around after Isis when she had visited before. He had been far more interested in the buttered scones that they'd had for tea.

"And, of course, Travers is one of the few people who would be able to come up with those confounded messages that are being painted up all over the place. Did you see what's been done to my sphinxes? Hieroglyphics all over them! They appeared the night before last – all the footmen have been trying to scrub the paint away, but it's still there. Oh, good heavens, where is that tea?" Lord Dacre muttered. "I do apologize, the house seems to be upside down these days. What with Isis ill, and half the servants giving notice because they think we're all cursed, it's a wonder I ever get anything to drink at all."

Fincham came in, looking rather flustered and carrying a tray. He was followed by a terrified young girl, who obviously wasn't used to waiting on visitors. Maisie suspected she might usually be a scullery maid – her hands were very red and chapped as if she'd been washing up. The girl set her silver tray down on the table with a clang, and the butler actually shuddered before hustling her out of the room.

"I'm so sorry, my lord. The cook is having hysterics after reading about the latest painted message in the newspapers. Mrs Binns seems to think that a man with the head of a vulture is going to eat her heart, my lord."

"Good Lord, Fincham," Lord Dacre muttered crossly. "Where on earth do they get this nonsense from? Absolute rubbish. Vultures! She may be confused about Anubis, I suppose. A jackal – like a dog, you know.

Perhaps I had better come and explain it to her."

The butler flinched. "I don't think that will be necessary, my lord," he said firmly, and Lord Dacre sat back.

"No, perhaps not. Fincham, has anyone taken tea to Miss Dacre?"

"I will do that directly, my lord."

"Shall I take it?" Maisie asked suddenly. "If you need to be downstairs seeing to the cook, Mr Fincham."

The butler was so harassed he didn't stop to think that Maisie's offer was rather strange, which was exactly what she had been hoping for. She hurried down to the kitchens after him to fetch the tray, and noticed the scullery maid looking at a recipe book and sniffing into a handkerchief. Obviously she was going to have to cook the dinner and she was not going to be up to it.

"Tell that Fincham to order in from a hotel," Maisie muttered in her ear, as she snatched up the tray and made for the stairs again. "His lordship won't notice, will he?"

Fincham had told her that Miss Dacre's room was down a passage to the right, but as Maisie came up the staircase and eyed the painted mummy case that was peering down over the banisters, she heard voices.

Whispers were hissing out from the passageway. It was amazing how many people didn't realize that whispering was easier to hear than simply speaking in a low voice, Maisie thought, as she padded quietly across the thick carpet and left the tray on top of a stone chest. It was probably some sort of ancient coffin, she realized guiltily, but she didn't think a tea tray would do it much harm.

She peered around the corner into the passageway, trying to listen in on the hissing voices.

"Pick out something really nasty..." It was a man's voice, sounding excited.

"I'm not sure we should, Max, dearest." That was Miss Dacre! Maisie leaned a little further around the corner of the passage. What on earth were they doing? And surely Miss Dacre was supposed to be desperately ill in bed, not having secret meetings in the corridor. Maisie could see them now. They were both standing by the wall, Isis in her nightgown with a shawl around her shoulders, and they were looking up at a framed papyrus.

“There, what does that say? Is it a curse?” Max asked, stabbing a finger at one of the painted symbols.

Miss Dacre frowned at it. “I’m not sure… It’s not that easy, you see. Sometimes the hieroglyphs are a letter, or … or an idea.

Or a name. It's not the same as English. I think that's the name of a priest."

"Well, can't he curse your father? Do hurry up, Isis, I want to deliver another message to your father tonight." He chuckled nastily, and Maisie shivered.

"I don't see why we need to paint another message," Miss Dacre protested. "If we frighten Papa much more, I'm worried it will affect his heart, Max. You know he's not strong. But I suppose we must," she added worriedly. "Poor Mr Travers. I shouldn't have said what I did about him courting me… I know you said we had to, but I never thought they'd actually arrest him. I just wanted to confuse the police… We have to paint up another message to prove that it wasn't him. But then, the doctors said Papa's heart was terribly weak…"

"Oh, he'll be fine," Max said airily. "Now please don't worry, darling, everything—Drat it, what's that?"

"The front doorbell! Oh, it's probably Dr Epps, I think Papa said he would call this afternoon. I must get back to my room!" Isis fluttered away up the passage, and Max stormed down towards Maisie, cursing. Maisie hurriedly ducked back and snatched up the tray, standing at the top of the stairs as though she had only just come up them. Max pushed past her with hardly a glance.

"Stupid, witless girl," he snarled, as he stomped down the stairs, and Maisie was quite sure that he didn't mean her. He'd hardly noticed she was there. But he couldn't be talking about Miss Dacre, could he? Not if they were in love. She stared after him, frowning. This was the most confusing case she had ever tried to solve. Gilbert Carrington, the private detective who was Maisie's hero, was famous for saying that motive was the most important thing. That it all came down to *why*. And at the moment, Maisie had absolutely no idea why at all. She shook her head and walked along the corridor to deliver the tea to Miss Dacre.

"Good afternoon, Miss. I've brought your tea."

"Who are you?" Miss Dacre asked, staring at Maisie in surprise. "Where's Margaret?"

Maisie bobbed a little curtsey and stared at the floor. Isis obviously hadn't recognized her, which was good. She didn't know if Lord Dacre had mentioned her to his daughter. "I'm not sure where she is, Miss. I was just visiting, and Fincham asked me to bring this up. I think some of the maids have left. Something about a curse?"

Miss Dacre's eyes widened a little. "Oh…" she said quietly. "Poor Margaret."

Maisie wondered if this was something Isis hadn't expected to happen. But just what *had* she been expecting? Maisie put the tea tray down on a little table by Miss Dacre's bed, slowly, so she could look at everything else that was on there. Several bottles of medicine and pills. Some books. A thermometer in a glass beaker. Miss Dacre's embroidery, which looked like it would be a fine lawn handkerchief when it was finished. She was stitching initials in the corner and a delicate border of leaves. Maisie recognized the stitching – she had seen Lord Dacre using a handkerchief just like that. So his daughter embroidered all his handkerchiefs for him?

Maisie smiled as she handed Miss Dacre her tea, but her mind was whirring. What did Miss Dacre actually want this strange plot to achieve? Only someone who loved their father would spend all their free time embroidering him handkerchiefs, surely? But she and Max were definitely behind the painted messages – Maisie had just watched them plotting the next one.

Were they both after the same thing, though? Miss Dacre seemed worried that they were going to scare her father too much, but Maisie had a feeling that frightening Lord Dacre to death might be exactly what Max wanted.

She handed Miss Dacre the sugar bowl, frowning to herself. Had Miss Dacre and Max stolen the scarab, too? Surely there weren't two sets of conspirators in the house – but that meant the rubies could be somewhere here, in this very room… Maisie's fingers itched to search it. But she couldn't, not properly. She would have to be sneaky, instead. Where would Miss Dacre have hidden those ruby eyes? There were so many places – under her pillow? No, too dangerous, the maids would find them when they changed the sheets. But Miss Dacre would want them close to her as she lay in bed.

Maisie's eyes widened as she spotted a little china pot on the table, next to the thermometer. It was just the right size for a pair of ruby eyes...

"Shall I tidy up a little, Miss?" she asked, looking at the messy piles of books and newspapers next to the bed.

"Oh, yes..." Miss Dacre said vaguely, sipping her tea. "But don't touch anything on the table, please." Maisie was almost sure that she glanced at the tiny pot as she spoke. "Was that the doctor at the front door, do you know?"

"I'm not sure, Miss," Maisie said, scooping up an armful of books. "Would you like me to go and see?"

"Yes… Yes, could you?" Miss Dacre was sitting up a little straighter, Maisie noticed.

Maisie bobbed her a curtsey, and walked to the door, pulling it almost closed behind her, but not quite. She stopped and peered back through the slit. Miss Dacre bounced upright as soon as she thought Maisie had gone and whipped the thermometer out of the glass beaker. Then she dipped it into the teapot and held it there.

Maisie shook her head disgustedly and retreated a little further down the passage, in case Miss Dacre should see her. She wasn't surprised to learn that Isis was trying to deceive the doctor. After all, she had seen her in the passage, looking perfectly healthy. The nervous collapse was just an act. But it was making Maisie cross now. Miss Dacre might not be frightened and worried, but her father certainly was, and poor Mr Travers was in a police cell. Whatever strange reasons Miss Dacre and Max had for this conspiracy, they had to be stopped.

Maisie knew she didn't have enough proof to convince Lord Dacre that it was his own daughter and cousin who had stolen the scarab. So she was just going to have make them prove it themselves.

She was still clutching one of the newspapers that had been on Miss Dacre's floor. As she stared down at it, trying to come up with a plan, the words "Disastrous Fire in London Street" caught her eye. It was an article about the fire she had witnessed herself, a couple of days before. All those poor people, clutching the treasures they'd saved from the flames. Maisie's mouth curled at the corner. If she was right, and Miss Dacre really did have those rubies hidden somewhere in her bedroom, then wouldn't she try to save them from a fire? They were so valuable – and she had cared enough about them to pull them out of the scarab.

Dacre House, despite being full of ancient artefacts, was very modern and lit with gas-mantle lamps everywhere. Maisie bit her upper lip nervously as she folded part of the newspaper into a long spill, and held it over one of the wall-mounted lamps. It burst into flame horribly fast, and Maisie dropped it on to a marble-topped table and fed it with more newspaper, until she had a smoky little blaze.

Then she wafted the smoke towards Miss Dacre's bedroom door, screamed

"Fire!" as loud as she could, and waited, hoping that she wasn't going to end up burning down Lord Dacre's house and all his precious Egyptian treasures. She really ought to have made sure she had a jug of water ready before she started this, Maisie thought, eyeing the burning paper anxiously and hoping it wasn't too close to the velvet curtains.

There were footsteps now, racing up the stairs, and pattering inside Miss Dacre's room. The fire was dying away to wisps of blackened paper already, and Maisie blew on it, hoping to raise a bit more smoke.

Professor Tobin and Lord Dacre came racing along the passageway just as Miss Dacre burst out of her room, with the little china pot clutched in one hand.

"Where's the fire? Are you hurt, Isis?" Lord Dacre yelled.

"I don't know..." Miss Dacre looked around wildly, and then caught sight of the papery ashes. "Is that it?" She glared at Maisie. "What on earth did you do? I thought you were going to see if the doctor had arrived."

"Maisie, are you all right?" Professor Tobin asked, panting. "Was it you that shouted?"

Maisie nodded. "I'm sorry if I gave you a

fright, Professor. That's all the fire there is," she said, pointing.

Then, as everyone stared at the ashes, she darted sideways and snatched the china pot out of Miss Dacre's hand, pulling off the lid. She tipped the rubies out on to the marble tabletop, where they glittered among the powdery ash.

Lord Dacre stared down at them, and then he turned and shooed away the servants, who were hurrying up with buckets of water. "A misunderstanding! So sorry! Er, Fincham, give everyone the evening off." Then he picked up the rubies with shaking fingers, and took his daughter by the elbow, leading her towards the stairs. "You had better come with us," he muttered to Maisie and Professor Tobin.

"Thank you for coming to rescue me, Professor," Maisie murmured, as they followed him.

"Was this all a clever trap, Maisie?"

Maisie sighed. "Yes. But now I wish I hadn't done it. Lord Dacre looks more upset than he ever was about the scarab. I suppose at least Mr Travers will be let out."

"If this really was Isis, then Leggy needed

to know. There must have been a reason…"
But even Professor Tobin looked pale and
horrified, and Maisie only felt worse.

Inside the library, Miss Dacre was sitting in an armchair by the fire, crying silently, and her father was gently wrapping a blanket around her knees.

"I'm not ill!" she sniffed. "It was all pretend. I'm perfectly well. You don't need to fuss over me, Papa!" But then she reached up and caught his hand. "When you heard that girl call fire, you came for me."

"Well, of course I did!"

"Not for the pharaoh's jewelled pendant first? Or that wonderful papyrus in the library? Or the crocodile armour?"

"Isis, dearest, of course not!" He ducked

his head. "I admit, once I was sure that you were safely outside, I might have gone back..."

"But you came for me first." She shook her head, disbelievingly. "I'm so sorry, Papa. Max said..."

"Where is Max?" Lord Dacre looked around worriedly. "Someone ought to tell the poor chap there isn't a fire after all."

"I'm afraid he's gone, Leggy." Professor Tobin snorted disapprovingly. "As we came running up the stairs, he left by the front door."

"He didn't even wait to see if I was safe?" Miss Dacre sat up straight, two patches of colour burning in her cheeks. "The wretch! He said he loved me!" She sniffed again, and dabbed her eyes on Lord Dacre's handkerchief. "He said he loved me far more than you did, Papa. That you only cared for your treasures. He said that you'd be off on another expedition soon. He told me that you were planning it, even when Dr Epps had said you mustn't. And I was so lonely when you went away! That's why I..." She hung her head miserably.

"You stole it – my scarab? But why?" her father said sadly.

"I should never have listened to him. And I hated that Max had to throw it away, but he said it was too risky to keep it in the house. I've felt so awful, seeing how upset you were. I just wanted you to stay at home, and not go off travelling and make yourself ill!"

"So you tried to frighten your father instead, even though you knew he had a weak heart?" Maisie said, stepping closer to Isis, her voice flat and cold.

Miss Dacre's pale blue eyes filled with tears. "It was terribly silly of me," she agreed. "But Max said..."

"How long do you think you would have lasted, once Max had frightened your father to death and then married you and got his hands on all the money?" Maisie said, and Miss Dacre stared at her in horror.

"He wouldn't..."

"I bet he would. He didn't exactly come rushing to save you from the fire, did he?"

"I'm so sorry," Miss Dacre whispered.

"I shall go and send a telegraph to the police, telling them to let Travers go at once," Professor Tobin said, heading for the door.

"Oh, poor Mr Travers!" Miss Dacre wailed. "I felt so dreadful when he was taken away!"

Lord Dacre patted her hand comfortingly, but Maisie rolled her eyes. She had never, ever met anyone so feeble. "So you should," she muttered. "The police will be here soon. You can tell them to go after Max Dacre instead. They just need to look out for someone with an idiotic little pointy beard."

"It's very fashionable!" Miss Dacre

protested, before she remembered that Max was a criminal who'd been trying to trick her into murdering her father. "Well. Yes, I suppose it is a little bit silly."

"A gold sovereign?" Gran eyed it admiringly. The gold coin was glinting on the little table in the professor's rooms. "I haven't seen one of those in quite a while, Maisie."

"It's well deserved, Mrs Hitchins," the professor said proudly. "Very well deserved. Your granddaughter was a marvel. Lord Dacre was most impressed." He smiled. "I shouldn't be surprised if he mentions your name to his smart friends, Maisie. You may find yourself with all sorts of high-society clients."

Maisie giggled. She couldn't really imagine them all coming calling at 31 Albion Street. She ran her fingers over the queen's head on the coin and sighed. It would be lovely to spend it. She could buy several new dresses, so that people like Isis didn't think she was scruffy and unimportant. But even though her purple dress was faded, it was still perfectly good. It kept her warm. She was thinking of those thin, grey-faced children down at the edge of the river.

A sovereign would buy them all warm clothes. Or hot meals for weeks. She would go and give it to them, she decided, a little sadly, the pretty dresses fading from her mind.

"And it was his daughter, all this time?" Gran asked, clicking her tongue disapprovingly.

The professor nodded. "The bond between a father and a daughter can be very special, Mrs Hitchins," he said, eyeing Maisie thoughtfully. "Lord Dacre hasn't just sent you the money. Look at the rest of your parcel." He held out her pendant and a piece of paper. "He must have managed to work out what it says."

Maisie took the necklace and the letter, and began to read.

My dear Miss Hitchins,

My daughter and I thank you for your brave and ingenious service. You will be glad to know that I will not be travelling to Egypt again. Instead, Isis and I are planning to work on my book, with the help of dear Mr Travers.

I have examined your pendant – a most meaningful gift from your own father. The lines are in fact a picture, as you suspected, and I have drawn them here more clearly, so that you can see they form an eye.

This is the eye of Horus, a god, and it is a symbol of good health and protection.

The message on the underside is a prayer for safety of a loved one. Your father may not have known what he was sending you, but I am sure that it is exactly as he would have wished.

With my most sincere thanks,

I remain,

Your servant,

Adolphus Tremayne Dacre

Maisie cupped her fingers tightly around the precious necklace and smiled. She was sure that Lord Dacre was right. It would be odd to have her father home again – very odd. But she liked the idea that even though he was far away, he was thinking about her and Gran.

She would write and tell him what it meant, although she wondered if somehow he already knew.

Maisie Hitchins
Maisie Hitchins
The Case of the Stolen Sixpence
HOLLY WEBB
Maisie Hitchins
The Case of the Vanishing Emerald
HOLLY WEBB
Maisie Hitchins
The Case of the Phantom Cat
HOLLY WEBB
Maisie Hitchins
HOLLY WEBB
Maisie Hitchins
The Case of the Secret Tunnel
HOLLY WEBB
Maisie Hitchins
The Case of the Spilled Ink
HOLLY WEBB
Maisie Hitchins
The Case of the Blind Beetle
HOLLY WEBB
Maisie Hitchins
The Case of the Weeping Mermaid
HOLLY WEBB

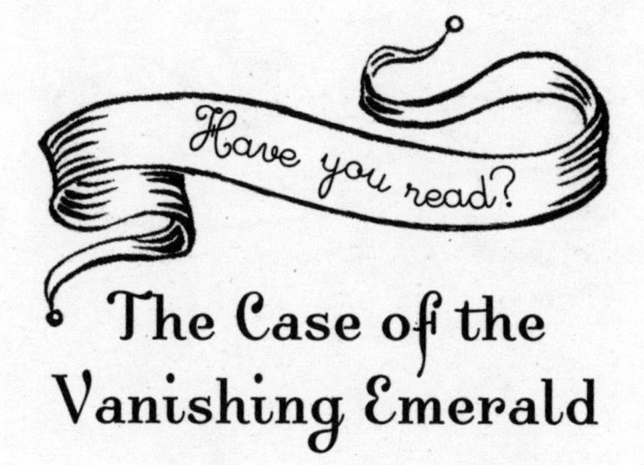

The Case of the Vanishing Emerald

When star-of-the-stage Sarah Massey comes to visit, Maisie senses a mystery. Sarah is distraught – her fiancé has given her a priceless emerald necklace and now it's gone missing. Maisie sets out to investigate, but nothing is what it seems in the theatrical world of make-believe...

The Case of the Phantom Cat

Maisie has been invited to the country as a companion for her best friend, Alice. But as soon as the girls arrive, they are warned that the manor house they're staying in is haunted. With Alice terrified by the strange goings-on, it's up to Maisie to prove there's no such thing as ghosts…

The Case of the Phantom Cat

Maisie has been invited to the country as a companion for her best friend, Alice. But as soon as the girls arrive, they are warned that the manor house they're staying in is haunted. With Alice terrified by the strange goings-on, it's up to Maisie to prove there's no such thing as ghosts…

eBook available

The Case of the Feathered Mask

Maisie loves to look at the amazing objects her friend Professor Tobin has collected on his travels around the world. But when a thief steals a rare and valuable wooden mask, leaving only a feather behind, Maisie realizes she has a new mystery on her hands…

The Case of the Secret Tunnel

Gran has a new lodger and Maisie suspects there's more to him than meets the eye. Fred Grange says he works for a biscuit company, but he is out at odd hours and knows nothing about biscuits! Determined to uncover the truth, Maisie is drawn into a mystery that takes her deep underground…

Find out more about Holly Webb
www.holly-webb.com